Richard Paul Evans

◆

The
Christmas
Box

◆

SIMON & SCHUSTER
New York London Toronto
Sydney Tokyo Singapore

Simon & Schuster
Rockefeller Center
1230 Avenue of the Americas
New York, NY 10020

Simon & Schuster and colophon are registered trademarks
of Simon & Schuster, Inc.

Designed by Pei Koay

Manufactured in the United States of America

10 9 8 7 6 5 4 3 2 1

Library of Congress Cataloging-In-Publication Data
Evans, Richard Paul.
The Christmas Box/Richard Paul Evans.
        p. cm
1. Christmas Stories, American.
  PS3555.V259C48   1995
813'.54—dc20   95-20026
        CIP
ISBN: 0-7432-3656-4

For information regarding special discounts for bulk purchases, please contact Simon &
Schuster Special Sales at 1-800-456-6798 or business@simonandschuster.com

For my sister Sue.
Whom I love and I miss.

Contents

◆

The
Christmas
Box

*No little girl could stop
the world to wait for me.*

—NATALIE MERCHANT

Chapter I

◆

THE WIDOW'S MANSION

*I*t may be that I am growing old in this world and have used up more than my share of allotted words and eager audiences. Or maybe I am just growing weary of a skeptical age that pokes and prods at my story much the same as a middle-school biology student pokes and prods through an anesthetized frog to determine what makes it live, leaving the poor creature dead in the end. Whatever the reason, I find that with each passing Christmas the story of the Christmas Box is told less and needed more. So I record it now for all future generations to accept or dismiss as seems them good. As for me, I believe. And it is, after all, my story.

My romantic friends, those who believe in Santa Claus in particular, have speculated that the ornamented brown Christmas Box was fashioned by Saint Nick himself from the trunk of the very first Christmas tree, brought in from the cold December snows so many seasons ago. Others believe that it was skillfully carved and polished from the hard and splintered wood from whose rough surface the Lord of Christmas had demonstrated the ultimate love for mankind. My wife, Keri, maintains that the magic of the box had nothing to do with its physical elements, but all to do with the contents that were hidden beneath its brass, holly-shaped hinges and silver clasps. Whatever the truth about the origin of the box's magic, it is the emptiness of the box that I will treasure most, and the memory of the Christmas season when the Christmas Box found me.

◆

I was born and raised in the shadow of the snow-clad Wasatch range on the east bench of the Salt Lake Valley. Just two months before my fourteenth birthday my father lost his job, and with promise of employment, we sold our home and migrated to the warmer, and more prosperous, climate of Southern California. There, with great disappointment, I came to expect a green Christmas almost as religiously as the local retailers. With the exception of one fleeting moment of glory as the lead in the school musical, my teenage years were uneventful and significant only to myself. Upon graduation from high school, I enrolled in college to learn the ways of business, and in the process learned the ways of life; met, courted, and married a fully matriculated, brown-eyed design student named Keri, who, not fifteen months from the ceremony, gave birth to a seven-pound-two-ounce daughter whom we named Jenna.

Neither Keri nor I ever cared much for the crowds of the big city, so when a few weeks before graduation we were informed of a business opportunity in my hometown, we jumped at the chance to return to the thin air and white winters of home. We had expended all but a small portion of our savings in the new venture and, as the new business's initial returns, albeit promising, were far from abundant, we learned the ways of thrift and frugality. In matters financial, Keri became expert at making much from little, so we rarely felt the extent of our deprivation. Except in the realm of lodging. The three of us needed more space than our cramped, one-bedroom apartment afforded. The baby's crib, which economics necessitated the use of in spite of the fact that our baby was now nearly four, barely fit in our bedroom, leaving less than an inch between it and our bed, which was already pushed up tightly against the far wall. The kitchen was no better, cluttered with Jenna's toy box, Keri's sewing hutch, and stacked cardboard boxes containing cases of canned foods. We joked that Keri could make clothing and dinner at the same time without ever leaving her seat. The topic of overcrowding had reached fever pitch in our household just seven weeks before Christmas and such was the frenzied state of our minds when the tale of the Christ-

mas Box really began, at the breakfast table in our little apartment, over
eggs over-easy, toast, and orange
juice.

"Look at this," Keri said, handing
me the classifieds:

Elderly lady with large Avenues home
seeks live-in couple for meal preparation, light housekeeping, and yard care.
Private quarters. Holidays off. Children/
infants welcome. 445–3989. Mrs. Parkin

I looked up from the paper.
"What do you think?" she asked.
"It's in the Avenues, so it has to be
large. It's close to the shop and it
really wouldn't be that much extra
trouble for me. What's one extra person to cook and wash for?" she asked
rhetorically. She reached over and
took a bite of my toast. "You're usually
gone in the evenings anyhow."

I leaned back in contemplation.

"It sounds all right," I said cautiously. "Of course, you never know what you might be getting into. My brother Mark lived in this old man's basement apartment. He used to wake Mark up in the middle of the night screaming at a wife who had been dead for nearly twenty years. Scared Mark to death. In the end he practically fled the place."

A look of disbelief spread across Keri's face.

"Well, it does say private quarters," I conceded.

"Anyway, with winter coming on, our heating bill is going to go through the roof in this drafty place and I don't know where the extra money will come from. This way we might actually put some money aside," Keri reasoned.

It was pointless to argue with such logic, not that I cared to. I, like Keri, would gladly welcome any change that would afford us relief from the cramped and cold quarters where we were presently residing. A few moments later Keri called to see if the apartment was still vacant and upon learning that it was, set up an appointment to meet with the owner that evening. I managed to leave work early and, following the directions given to Keri by a man at the house, we made our way through the gaily lit downtown business district and to the tree-lined streets leading up the foothills of the Avenues.

The Parkin home was a resplendent, red-block Victorian mansion with ornate cream-and-raspberry wood trim and dark green shingles. On the west side of the home, a rounded bay window supported a second-story veranda balcony that overlooked the front yard. The balcony, like the main floor porch, ran the length of the exterior upheld by large, ornately lathed beams and a decorative, gold-leafed frieze. The wood was freshly painted and well kept. A sturdy brick chimney rose from the center of the home amid wood and wrought-iron spires that shot up decorously. Intricate latticework gingerbreaded the base of the house, hidden here and there by neatly trimmed evergreen shrubs. A cobblestone driveway wound up the front of the home, encircling a black marble fountain that lay iced over and surrounded by a snow-covered retaining wall.

I parked the car near the front steps, and we climbed the porch to the home's double door entryway. The doors were beautifully carved and inlaid with panes of glass etched with intricate floral patterns. I rang the bell and a man answered.

"Hello, you must be the Evanses."

"We are," I confirmed.

"MaryAnne is expecting you. Please come in."

We passed in through the entry, then through a second set of doors of equal magnificence leading into the home's marbled foyer. I have found that old homes usually have an olfactory presence to them, and though not often pleasant, unmistakenly distinct. This home was no exception, though the scent was a tolerably pleasant combination of cinnamon and kerosene. We walked down a wide corridor with frosted walls. Kerosene sconces, now wired for electric lights, dotted the walls and cast dramatic lighting the length of the hall.

"MaryAnne is in the back parlor," the man said.

The parlor lay at the end of the corridor, entered through an elaborate cherry-wood door casing. As we entered the room, an attractive silver-haired woman greeted us from behind a round marble-topped rosewood table. Her attire mimicked the elaborate, rococo decor that surrounded her.

"Hello," she said cordially. "I am MaryAnne Parkin. I'm happy that you have come. Please have a seat." We sat around the table, our attention drawn to the beauty and wealth of the room.

"Would you care for some peppermint tea?" she offered. In front of her sat an embossed, silver-plated tea service. The teapot was pear-shaped, with decorative bird feathers etched into the sterling body. The spout emulated the graceful curves of a crane's neck and ended in a bird's beak.

"No, thank you," I replied.

"I'd like some," said Keri.

She handed Keri a cup and poured it to the brim. Keri thanked her.

"Are you from the city?" the woman asked. "I was born and raised here," I replied. "But we've just recently moved up from California."

"My husband was from California," she said. "The Santa Rosa area." She studied our eyes for a spark of recognition. "Anyway, he's gone now. He passed away some fourteen years ago."

"We're sorry to hear that," Keri said politely.

"It's quite all right," she said. "Fourteen years is a long time. I've grown quite accustomed to being alone." She set down her cup and straightened herself up in the plush wingback chair.

"Before we begin the interview I would like to discuss the nature of the arrangement. There are a few items that you will find I am rather insistent about. I need someone to provide meals. You have a family, I assume you can cook." Keri nodded. "I don't eat breakfast, but I expect brunch to be served at eleven and dinner at six. My washing should be done twice a week, preferably Tuesday and Friday, and the beddings should be washed at least once a week. You are welcome to use the laundry facilities to do your own washing any time you find convenient. As for the exterior," she said, looking at me, "the lawn needs to be cut once a week, except when there is snow, at which time the walks, driveway, and back porch need to be shoveled and salted as the climate dictates. The other landscaping and home maintenance I hire out and would not require your assistance. In exchange for your service you will have the entire east wing in which to reside. I will pay the heating and light bills and any other household expenses. All that is required of you is attention to the matters we have discussed. If this arrangement sounds satisfactory to you, then we may proceed."

We both nodded in agreement.

"Good. Now if you don't mind, I have a few questions I'd like to ask."

"No, not at all," Keri said.

"Then we'll begin at the top." She donned a pair of silver-framed bifocals, lifted from the table a small handwritten list, and began the interrogation.

"Do either of you smoke?"

"No," said Keri.

"Good. I don't allow it in the home. It spoils the draperies. Drink to excess?" She glanced over to me.

"No," I replied.

"Do you have children?"

"Yes, we have one. She's almost four years old," said Keri.

"Wonderful. She's welcome anywhere in the house except this room. I would worry too much about my porcelains," she said, smiling warmly. Behind her I could see a black walnut étagère with five steps, each supporting a porcelain figurine. She continued. "Have you a fondness for loud music?" Again she looked my way.

"No," I answered correctly. I took this more as a warning than a prerequisite for cohabitation.

"And what is your current situation in life?"

"I'm a recent college graduate with a degree in business. We moved to Salt Lake City to start a formal-wear rental business."

"Such as dinner jackets and tuxedos?" she asked.

"That's right," I said.

She took mental note of this and nodded approvingly.

"And references." She glanced up over her bifocals. "Have you references?"

"Yes. You may contact these people," said Keri, handing her a scrawled-out list of past landlords and employers. She meticulously studied the list, then laid it down on the end table, seemingly impressed with the preparation. She looked up and smiled.

"Very well. If your references are satisfactory, I think we may make an arrangement. I think it is best that we initiate a forty-five-day trial period, at the end of which time we may ascertain if the situation is mutually favorable. Does that sound agreeable?"

"Yes, ma'am," I replied.

"You may call me Mary. My name is MaryAnne, but my friends call me Mary."

"Thank you, Mary."

"Now I've done all the talking. Have you any questions that I might answer?"

"We'd like to see the apartment," Keri said.

"Of course. The quarters are up-stairs in the east wing. Steve will lead you up. They are unlocked. I think you will find that they have been tastefully furnished."

"We do have some furniture of our own," I said. "Is there some extra space where we could store it?"

"The doorway to the attic is at the end of the upstairs hall. Your things will be very convenient there," she replied.

I helped myself to a cracker from the silver tray. "Was that your son who answered the door?" I asked.

She took another sip of her tea. "No. I have no children. Steve is an old friend of mine from across the street. I hire him to help maintain the home." She paused thoughtfully for another sip of tea and changed the subject. "When will you be prepared to move in?"

"We need to give our landlord two weeks notice, but we could move in anytime," I said.

"Very good. It will be nice to have someone in the house for the holidays."

Chapter II

◆

THE
CHRISTMAS BOX

*I*t is not my intent to launch upon a lengthy or sanctimonious dissertation on the social significance and impact of the lowly box, well deserved as it may be. But as a box plays a significant role in our story, please allow me the indulgence of digression. From the inlaid jade-and-coral jewelry boxes of the Orient to the utilitarian salt boxes of the Pennsylvania Dutch, the allure of the box has transcended all cultural and geographical boundaries of the world. The cigar box, the snuff box, the cash box, jewelry boxes more ornate than the treasure they hold, the ice box, and the candle box. Trunks, long rectangular boxes covered with cowhide, stretched taut, and pounded with brass studs to a wooden frame. Oak boxes, sterling boxes; to the delight of the women, hat boxes and shoe boxes; and to the delight of all enslaved by a sweet tooth, candy boxes. The human life cycle no less than evolves around the box; from the open-topped box called a bassinet, to the pine box we call a coffin, the box is our past and, just as assuredly, our future. It should not surprise us then that the lowly box plays such a significant role in the first Christmas story. For Christmas began in a humble, hay-filled box of splintered wood. The Magi, wise men who had traveled far to see the infant king, laid treasure-filled boxes at the feet of that holy child. And in the end, when He had ransomed our sins with His blood, the Lord of Christmas was laid down in a box of stone. How fitting that each Christmas season brightly wrapped boxes skirt the pine boughs of Christmas trees around the world. And more fitting that I learned of Christmas through a Christmas Box.

◆

We determined to settle into the home as soon as possible, so the following Saturday I borrowed a truck from work and my brother-in-law, Barry, the only relative living within two hundred miles, came to help us move. The two of us hauled things out to the truck, while Keri wrapped dishes in newspaper and packed them in boxes, and Jenna played contentedly in the front room, oblivious to the gradual disappearance of our belongings. We managed to load most of our things, which were not great in number, into the truck. The rest of the boxes were piled into our Plymouth—a large pink-and-chrome coupe with graceful curves, majestic tail fins, and a grill resembling the wide, toothy grin of a Cheshire cat. When we had finished clearing out the apartment the four of us squeezed into the cargo-laden vehicles and together drove off to our new residence in the Avenues. I parked the car out front and met Barry in the driveway.

"Just pull it around back," I shouted, guiding the truck with hand gestures. He backed around to the rear of the house, pulled the parking brake, and hopped out.

"You're moving into a mansion?" he asked enviously.

"Your blue-blooded sister found it," I replied.

I released the tailgate while Barry untied the straps securing the canvas tarpaulin we had used to cover the load.

"Here, give me a hand with this wicker chest. We'll take it straight up to the attic." Barry grabbed hold of the handle at one end of the chest and we lifted it down from the truck's bed.

"Only one person lives in this house?" he asked.

"Four now, counting the three of us," I replied.

"With all this room why doesn't her family just move in with her?"

"She doesn't have any family. Her husband died and she doesn't have any children."

Barry surveyed the ornate Victorian facade. "There's bound to be a lot of history in a place like this," he said thoughtfully.

We made our way up the stairs, through the kitchen, down the hall, then up the attic steps. We set the chest down at the top of the landing to catch our breath.

"We'd better make some room up here before we bring the rest of the things up," Barry suggested.

I agreed. "Let's clear a space against that wall so we can keep our things all in one place." We began the chore of rearranging the attic.

"I thought you said she didn't have any children," Barry said.

"She doesn't," I replied.

"Why is there a cradle up here then?" Barry stood near a dusty draped sheet revealing the form of a shrouded cradle.

"Maybe she's storing it for someone," I suggested.

I lifted a small stack of boxes and set them aside. "I haven't seen one of these for a while," I said, displaying my own discovery.

"What is it?"

"A tie press. It must have been her husband's."

Barry hoisted a large portrait of a man with a handlebar mustache posing stoically for the picture. The portrait was set in an elaborate gold-leafed frame.

"Look," he said, "their banker." We laughed.

"Hello, look at this," I said, as I gently lifted what looked to be an heirloom. It was an ornate wooden box of burled walnut, intricately carved and highly polished. It was about ten inches wide, fourteen inches long, and a half foot deep, large enough for a sheet of stationery to lie flat inside. It had two large brass hinges crafted in the form of holly leaves. Two leather straps ran horizontally across the lid and buckled securely into silver clasps on each side. The lid had a skilled and detailed etching of the Nativity. Barry walked over for a closer look.

"I've never seen anything like it," I said.

"What is it?" Barry asked.

"A Christmas Box. For storing Christmas things in. Cards, baubles, things like that." I shook it gently. There was no rattle.

"How old do you think it is?" Barry asked.

"Turn-of-the-century," I speculated. "See the craftsmanship?"

While he took a closer look, I cast my eyes around the room at the work remaining to be done.

"We better get on with this," I lamented. "I have a lot of work to catch up on tonight."

I set the box aside and we went back to organizing space for our things. It was dark outside by the time we finished unloading the truck. Keri had long finished unpacking the kitchen boxes and dinner was waiting for us on the table when we came down.

"Well, Sister, what do you think of your new home?" Barry asked.

"I could get used to all this room," Keri said, "and the furniture."

"You should see some of the things up in the attic," I said.

"Mom, how will Santa find our new house?" Jenna asked anxiously.

"Oh, Santa's elves keep track of these things," she assured her.

"The trick will be how Santa's reindeer will land on the roof without impaling themselves," I joked.

Keri cast a sideways glance toward me.

"What's impaling?" asked Jenna.

"Never mind your dad, he's just teasing."

Barry laughed. "Aren't you supposed to be making dinner for the lady?" he asked.

"We officially begin our arrangement on Monday. In fact, she is making dinner for us tomorrow. At least she invited us to dine with her."

"Is that right?" I asked.

"She was up here just before the two of you came down."

"This should be interesting," I decided.

We finished the meal and, after thanking Barry profusely for his help, we cleared away the dishes. Then I dove into a pile of receipts and ledgers, while Keri put Jenna to bed.

"Can Daddy read me a story?" she asked.

"Not tonight, honey. Daddy has a lot of work to do."

"It doesn't have to be a long one," she pleaded.

"Not tonight, honey. Some other time."

A disappointed child was tucked under the covers and went to sleep yearning for "some other time."

Chapter III

◆

THE
BIBLE BOX

Sunday was not proclaimed the "day of rest" by a mother with a family to ready for church, but such is the irony of piousness. Upon our return home at the conclusion of the day's "churching," we reveled in the discovery of a glorious new lifestyle. In our last apartment we had had such little space we found ourselves looking for ways to spend our Sunday afternoons outside the home. Now we defiantly spread our things, and ourselves, throughout our quarters. I napped in front of the drawing room fireplace while Keri read in the bedroom and Jenna played quietly in the nursery. What we may have lost in family togetherness we more than made up for in sanity.

At quarter to six Keri woke me, and after washing up, we descended the stairs to Mary's dining room. It smelled wonderfully of roast beef and gravy and freshly baked rolls. The dining room was spacious and, in typical Victorian style, the floor was covered with a colorful Persian rug that stopped short of the walls, leaving a border of the polished hardwood floor exposed. The room was built around a large, rectangular, white-laced dining table. A Strauss crystal chandelier hung from the ceiling directly above the center of the table, suspended above a vase of freshly cut flowers. The east wall had an elaborate built-in china closet displaying the home's exquisite porcelain dinnerware. On the opposite wall was a fireplace, as ornately carved as the parlor fireplace, but of lighter wood. The mantel extended to the ceiling, and the firebox and hearth were tiled in marbled blue-and-white patterns. To either side of the fireplace were walnut side chairs with Gothic carved backs and tucked haircloth upholstery.

Mary met us at the doorway and thanked us graciously for joining her.

"I'm so glad that you could come!" she said.

"The pleasure is ours," I assured her.

"You really shouldn't have gone to so much trouble," said Keri.

Mary was a hostess of the highest order and would not feel the affair worthwhile had she not gone to a lot of trouble.

"It was no trouble at all," she said instinctively.

The place settings were immaculate and beautiful, and the china plates were trimmed in 24 karat gold.

"Please sit down," she urged, motioning us to some chairs. We took our seats and waited for her to join us.

"I always pray before I eat," she said. "Would you please join me?"

We bowed our heads.

"Dear Lord, thank you for this bounty which we have during this blessed Christmas season. Thank you for these new friends. Please bless them in their needs and their desires. Amen."

We lifted our heads.

"Thank you," I said.

Mary uncovered a woven basket of steaming rolls, broke them apart, and placed one on each of our plates. She then filled our goblets with water and the food-laden platters were passed around the table.

"So how are your quarters?" Mary asked. "Have you moved in all your things?"

"We have," Keri replied.

"There was enough room in the attic? I was afraid it might be a little cramped."

"Plenty," I assured her. "We don't own much furniture." I lifted another spoonful from my plate then added, "You really have some beautiful things up there."

She smiled. "Yes. That's mostly my David's doing. David loved to collect things. As a businessman, he traveled all around the world. He always brought something back from each journey. In his spare time he became very knowledgeable about furniture and antiques. A few years before he died he had started collecting Bibles."

I bobbed my head in interest.

"See this Bible over here?" she said. She motioned to a large, leather-bound book sitting alone on a black lacquer papier-mâché table inlaid with mother-of-pearl. "That Bible is over two hundred and fifty years old. It was one of David's favorite finds," she shared joyously. "He brought it back from Britain. Collectors call it the 'wicked' Bible. In the first printing the printer made an error, and in Exodus they omitted the word 'not' from the seventh commandment. It reads 'Thou shalt commit adultery.' "

"That's deplorable," Keri chuckled.

Mary laughed out loud. "It's true," she said. "After supper you're welcome to look it up. The British crown fined the printer three hundred pounds for the mistake."

"That was a costly mistake," I said.

"It was a very popular version," she

said, smiling mischievously. "In the front parlor is a French Bible with what they call fore-edge painting. If you fan the pages back there is a watercolor of the Nativity. It was a unique art form of the period. Upstairs in the attic is a Bible box that David bought for it, but I think the book is so beautiful that I leave it out."

"The Christmas Box," I said.

She looked surprised at my familiarity with the box.

"Yes, there is a Nativity scene etched in the wood—of the Madonna and the Baby Jesus."

"I saw it up there. It's very beautiful."

"It's not from France, though," she explained. "I believe it was from Sweden. Fine box-making was an art in the Scandinavian countries. When David passed away I received not a few requests to purchase the

Bibles. Except for the Bible I donated to the church, and the three that I still have, I sold the rest. I just couldn't part with these three. David took such joy in them. They were his favorite treasures."

"Where is the third Bible?" I asked.

"I keep it in the den, for my personal reading. I'm sure there are some collectors that would have my head for doing so, but it has special significance to me." She looked down at Jenna.

"But enough of these old things, tell me about your sweet little three-year-old," she said kindly.

Jenna had been sitting quietly, cautiously sampling her food, largely ignored by all of us. She looked up shyly.

"Jenna is going to be four in January," Keri said.

"I'm going to be this many," Jenna said proudly, extending a hand with one digit inverted.

"That is a wonderful age!" Mary exclaimed. "Do you like your new home?"

"I like my bed," she said matter-of-factly.

"She's glad to get out of her crib," Keri explained. "We didn't have room in our last apartment for a bed. She was devastated when she found out that she was the only one in her dance class who slept in a crib."

Mary smiled sympathetically.

"Oh, speaking of dance," Keri remembered, turning to me, "Jenna's Christmas dance recital is this Saturday. Can you make it?"

I frowned. "I'm afraid not. Saturday is going to be a busy day at the shop with all the December weddings and Christmas formals."

"It must be a very busy time of the year for your type of business," Mary offered.

"It is," I replied, "but it drops off in January."

She nodded politely then turned to Keri. "Well, I, for one, am glad that Jenna likes it here. And, if you're wanting for company, I would love to take Richard's place at that dance recital."

"You are more than welcome to join us," Keri said. Jenna smiled.

"Then it's a date. And," she said, looking at Jenna, "for the little dancer, I made some chocolate Christmas pudding. Would you like some?"

Jenna smiled hungrily.

"I hope you don't mind," Mary said, turning to us. "She hasn't finished her supper."

"Of course not," Keri said. "That was very thoughtful of you."

Mary excused herself from the table and returned carrying a tray of crystal bowls filled with steaming pudding. She served Jenna first.

"This is very good," I said, plunging a spoonful into my mouth.

"Everything is delicious," Keri said. "Thank you."

The conversation lulled while we enjoyed the dessert. Jenna was the first to break the silence.

"I know why flies come in the house," she announced unexpectedly.

We looked at her curiously.

"You do?" Mary asked.

Jenna looked at us seriously. "They come in to find their friends . . ."

We all stifled a laugh, as the little girl was in earnest.

". . . and then we kill them."

Keri and I looked at each other and burst out laughing.

"My, you are a little thinker," Mary said. She chuckled, then leaned over and gave Jenna a hug.

"I'd like to propose a toast," Mary said. She raised a crystal glass of wine. Following Mary's lead we poured our glasses half full of the rose liquid and held them in the air.

"To a new friendship and a wonderful Christmas."

"Hear, hear," I said emphatically.

"A wonderful Christmas," Keri repeated.

The rest of the evening was spent in pleasant conversation, punctuated with laughter. When we had finished eating, we lavishly praised Mary for a wonderful meal and transported the dishes to the kitchen. Mary firmly insisted on cleaning up the dishes herself, so reluctantly we left her to the chore and returned upstairs to our wing.

"I feel like I've known her all my life," Keri said.

"Like a grandmother," I observed.

Jenna smiled and raced up the stairs ahead of us.

◆

The ritual of cohabitation took on a natural and casual openness welcomed by all. It soon became clear to Keri and me that Mary had solicited a family to move in with her more for the sake of "family" than real physical need. She could easily have hired servants, as there obviously had been in the past, and she seemed to trouble herself immensely to make our stay amiable, to the extent of hiring out any chore that Keri or I might find overly tedious or time-consuming, except when said chore would invoke a vicarious act of a familial nature. Bringing home the Christmas tree was such an occasion. Mary, upon finding the largest, most perfectly shaped tree in the lot, offered to purchase a second pine for our quarters. She was absolutely delighted when Keri suggested that we might all enjoy sharing the same tree together. We brought the tree home and after much fussing, the fresh scent of evergreen permeated the den. Not surprisingly, the room became a favorite place for us to congregate after supper. We enjoyed Mary's company as much as she desired ours, and Jenna accepted her readily as a surrogate grandmother.

◆

Some people were born to work for others. Not in a mindless, servile way—rather, they simply work better in a set regimen of daily tasks and functions. Others were born of the entrepreneurial spirit and enjoy the demands of self-determination and the roll of the dice. Much to my detriment, I was born of the latter spirit. Frankly, that spirit was just as potent a draw to return to my hometown as the quaint streets and white-capped mountains I had grown up loving. As I said before, Keri and I had left Southern California for the opportunity to operate a formal-wear business. Though formal-wear rental is quite common now, at the time it was new and untested and therefore exciting. The opportunity came by way of a friend who found himself in a small town just north of Salt Lake City, called Bountiful, for a wedding. That is when he met my future partner, an enterprising tailor who had begun leasing elaborate bridal gowns, and soon discovered a greater need for suitable accoutrements for the bride's and bridesmaids' counterparts.

As necessity is the mother of profit, he began renting a line of men's dinner jackets with great success. It was at this time that my friend, while dressed in one of those suits, had, unbeknownst to me, engaged the proprietor in a lengthy discussion on the state and future of his business. Having been impressed with expectations of my marketing prowess, the owner called me directly and after many long-distance phone conversations offered to sell me a portion of the new company in exchange for my expertise and a small cash outlay, which Keri and I managed to scrape together. The opportunity was all we could have hoped for, and the business showed signs of great promise.

Under my direction, we increased our market by producing picture catalogs of our suits and sending them to dressmakers and wedding halls outside of the metropolitan area. They became the retailers of our suits, which they rented to their clientele, and received no small commission in the transaction. The paperwork of this new venture was enormous and complex, but the success of my ideas consumed me and I found myself gradually drawn away from the comparatively relaxed environment of home. In modern business vernacular, there is a popular term: "opportunity costs." The term is based on the assumption that since all resources, mainly time and money, are limited, the successful businessman weighs all ventures based on what opportunities are to be lost in the transaction. Perhaps if I had seen my daughter's longing eyes staring back at me from the gold-plated scales, I would have rethought my priorities. I adroitly rationalized my absence from home on necessity and told myself that my family would someday welcome the sacrifice by feasting, with me, on the fruits of my labors. In retrospect, I should have tasted those fruits for bitterness a little more often.

Chapter IV

◆

THE DREAM,
THE ANGEL,
AND THE LETTER

I don't recall the exact night when the dreams began. The angel dreams. It should be stated that I am a believer in angels, though not the picture-book kind with wings and harps. Such angelic accoutrements seem as nonsensical to me as devils sporting horns and carrying pitchforks. To me, angel wings are merely symbolic of their role as divine messengers. Notwithstanding my rather dogmatic opinions on the matter, the fact that the angel in my dream descended from the sky with outspread wings did not bother me. In fact, the only thing I found disturbing at all about the dream was its frequent recurrence and the dream's strange conclusion. In the dream I find myself alone in a large open field. The air is filled with soft, beautiful strains of music flowing as sweet and melodic as a mountain brook. I look up and see an angel with wings outspread descending gradually from heaven. Then, when we are not an arm's length removed, I look into its cherubic face, its eyes turn up toward heaven, and the angel turns to stone.

Though I have vague recollections of the dream haunting my sleep more than once after we moved into the Parkin home, it seemed to have grown clearer and more distinct with each passing slumber. This night it was alive, rich in color and sound and detail, occupying my every thought with its surrealism. I awoke suddenly, expecting all traces of the nocturnal vision to vanish with my consciousness, but it didn't. This night the music remained. A soft, silvery tune plucked sweetly as a lullaby. A lullaby of unknown origin.

Except tonight the music had an origin.

I sat up in bed, listening intently while my eyes adjusted to the darkness. I found the flashlight kept in the pine nightstand next to our bed, pulled on a terry-cloth robe, and walked quietly from the room, following the music. I felt my way down the hall past the nursery where I stopped and looked in at Jenna. She lay fast asleep, undisturbed by the tones. I followed the music to the end of the hall, pausing where the melody seemed to have originated, from behind the attic door. I grasped the handle and opened the door slowly. The flashlight illuminated the room, creating long, creeping shadows. Apprehensively, I climbed the stairs toward the music. The room was still and, except for the music, life-less. As I panned the room with the light, my heart quickened. The cradle was uncovered. The dusty, draped sheet that had concealed it now lay crumpled at its base on the attic floor. Anxiously, I continued my examina-tion, until I had centered the light on the source of the enchanted dis-turbance. It was the ornate heirloom box that Barry and I had discovered the afternoon that we had moved in our belongings. The Christmas Box. I hadn't known at the time it was capa-ble of music. How odd it should start playing in the middle of the night. I looked around once more to be sure that I was alone, then balanced the flashlight on one end so that its beam illuminated the rafters and lit the whole attic. I lifted the box and inspected it for a lever with which to turn off the music. The box was dusty and heavy and appeared just as we had seen it a few days previous. I inspected it more closely but could find no key and no spring, in fact no mechanism of any type. It was simply a wooden box. I unclasped the silver buckle and opened the lid slowly. The music stopped. I moved the flashlight close to examine the box. Inside lay several parchment documents. I reached in and lifted the top page. It was a letter. A handwritten letter, brittle with age and slightly yellowed. I held it near the flashlight to read. The handwriting was beautiful and disciplined.

December 6, 1914

My Beloved One,

I stopped. I have never been one to revel in the intrusion of another's privacy, much less inclined to read someone else's correspondence. Why then I was unable to resist reading the letter is as much a mystery to me as was the parchment itself. So strong was the compulsion that I finished the letter without so much as a second thought into the matter:

How cold the Christmas snows seem this year without you. Even the warmth of the fire does little but remind me of how I wish you were again by my side. I love you. How I love you.

I did not know why the letter beckoned me or even what significance it carried. Who was this Beloved One? Was this Mary's writing? It had been written nearly twenty years before her husband had passed away. I set the letter back in the box and shut the lid. The music did not start up again. I left the attic and returned to my bed pondering the contents of the letter. The mystery as to why the Christmas Box had started playing music, even how it had played music, remained, for the night, unanswered.

The next morning I explained the episode to an only slightly interested wife.

"So you didn't hear anything last night?" I asked. "No music?"

"No," Keri answered, "but you know I'm a pretty heavy sleeper."

"This is really strange," I said, shaking my head.

"So you heard a music box. What's so strange about that?"

"It was more than that," I explained. "Music boxes don't work that way. Music boxes play when you open them. This one stopped playing when I opened it. And the strangest part is that there didn't appear to be any mechanism to it."

"Maybe it was your angel making the music," she teased.

"Maybe it was," I said eerily. "Maybe this is one of those mystical experiences."

"How do you even know the music was coming from the box?" she asked skeptically.

"I'm sure of it," I said. I looked up and noticed the time. "Darn, I'm going to be late and I'm opening up today." I threw on my overcoat and started for the door.

Keri stopped me. "Aren't you going to kiss Jenna good-bye?" she asked incredulously. I ran back to the nursery to give Jenna a kiss.

I found her sitting in a pile of shredded paper with a pair of round-edged children's scissors in hand.

"Dad, can you help me cut these?" she asked.

"Not now, honey, I'm late for work."

The corners of her mouth pulled downward in disappointment.

"When I get home," I hastily promised. She sat quietly as I kissed her on the head.

"I've got to go. I'll see you tonight." I dashed out of the room, nearly forgetting the lunch which Keri had set by the door, and made my way through the gray, slushy streets to the formalwear shop.

◆

Each day, as the first streaks of dawn spread across the blue winter morning sky, Mary could be found in the front parlor, sitting comfortably in a posh, overstuffed Turkish chair, warming her feet in front of the fireplace. In her lap lay the third Bible. The one that she had kept. This morning ritual dated decades back but Mary could tell you the exact day it had begun. It was her "morning constitutional for the spirit," she had told Keri.

During the Christmas season she would read at length the Christmas stories of the Gospels, and it was here that she welcomed the small, uninvited guest.

"Well, good morning, Jenna," Mary said.

Jenna stood at the doorway, still clothed in the red-flannel nightshirt in which she almost always slept. She looked around the room then ran to Mary. Mary hugged her tightly.

"What are you reading? A story?" Jenna asked.

"A Christmas story," Mary said. Jenna's eyes lit up. She crawled onto Mary's lap and looked for pictures of reindeer and Santa Claus.

"Where are the pictures?" she asked. "Where's Santa Claus?"

Mary smiled. "This is a different kind of Christmas story. This is the first Christmas story. It's about the baby Jesus."

Jenna smiled. She knew about Jesus.

"Mary?"

"Yes, sweetheart?"

"Will Daddy be here at Christmas?"

"Why of course, dear," she assured. She brushed the hair back from Jenna's face and kissed her forehead. "You miss him, don't you?"

"He's gone a lot."

"Starting a new business takes a lot of work and a lot of time."

Jenna looked up sadly. "Is work better than here?"

"No. No place is better than home."

"Then why does Daddy want to be there instead of here?"

Mary paused thoughtfully. "I guess sometimes we forget," she answered and pulled the little girl close.

◆

With the approach of the holidays, business grew increasingly busy, and though we welcomed the revenue, I found myself working long days and returning home late each night. In my frequent absence, Keri had established the habit of sharing supper with Mary in the downstairs den. They had even adopted the ritual of sharing an after-dinner cup of peppermint tea near the fire. Afterward Mary would follow Keri into the kitchen and help clean up the supper dishes, while I, if home by this time, would remain in the den and finish the day's books. Tonight the snow fell softly outside, contrasted by the sputtering and hissing of the warm fire crackling in the fireplace. Jenna had been sent up to bed, and as Keri cleared the table, I remained behind, diving into a catalog of new-fashioned cummerbunds and matching band ties. Tonight Mary also remained behind, still sitting in the antique chair from which she always took her tea. Though she usually followed Keri into the kitchen, sometimes, after she had finished her tea, she would doze quietly in her chair until we woke her and helped her to her room.

Mary set down her tea, pushed herself up, and walked over to the cherry wood bookshelf. She pulled a book from a high shelf, dusted it lightly, and handed it to me.

"Here is a charming Christmas tale. Read this to your little one." I took the book from her outstretched arm and examined the title, *Christmas Every Day* by William Dean Howells.

"Thank you, Mary, I will." I smiled at her, set the book down, and went back to my catalog. Her eyes never left me.

"No, right now. Read it to her now," she coaxed. Her voice was fervent, wavering only from her age. I laid my text down, examined the book again, then looked back up into her calm face. Her eyes shone with the importance of her request.

"All right, Mary."

I rose from the table and walked up into Jenna's room, wondering when I would catch up on my orders and what magic this old book contained to command such urgency. Upstairs Jenna lay quietly in the dark.

"Still awake, honey?" I asked.

"Daddy, you forgot to tuck me in tonight."

I switched on the light. "I did, didn't I. How about a bedtime story?"

She jumped up in her bed with a smile that filled the tiny room. "What story are you going to tell?" she asked.

"Mary gave me this book to read to you."

"Mary has good stories, Dad."

"Then it should be a good one," I said. "Does Mary tell you stories often?"

"Every day."

I sat on the edge of the bed and opened the old book. The spine was brittle and cracked a little as it opened. I cleared my throat and started reading aloud.

The little girl came into her papa's study, as she always did Saturday morning before breakfast, and asked for a story. He tried to beg off that morning, for he was very busy, but she would not let him . . .

"That's like you, Dad. You're real busy too," Jenna observed.

I grinned at her. "Yeah, I guess so." I continued reading.

"Well, once there was a little pig—" The little girl put her hand over his mouth and stopped him at the word. She said she had heard the pig stories till she was perfectly sick of them.

"Well, what kind of story shall I tell, then?"

"About Christmas. It's getting to be the season, it's past Thanksgiving already."

"It seems to me," argued her papa, "that I've told as often about Christmas as I have about little pigs."

"No difference! Christmas is more interesting."

Unlike her story's counterpart, Jenna was long asleep before I finished the tale. Her delicate lips were drawn in a gentle smile, and I pulled the covers up tightly under her chin. Peace radiated from the tiny face. I lingered a moment, knelt down near her bed and kissed her on the cheek, then walked back down to finish my work.

I returned to the den to find the lavish drapes drawn tight, and the two women sitting together in the dim, flickering light of the fireplace talking peacefully. The soothing tones of Mary's voice resonated calmly through the room. She looked up to acknowledge my entrance.

"Richard, your wife just asked the most intriguing question. She asked which of the senses I thought was most affected by Christmas."

I sat down at the table.

"I love everything about this season," she continued. "But I think what I love most about Christmas are its sounds. The bells of street-corner Santa Clauses, the familiar Christmas records on the phonograph, the sweet, untuned voices of Christmas carolers. And the bustling downtown noises. The crisp crinkle of wrapping paper and department store sacks and the cheerful Christmas greetings of strangers. And then there are the Christmas stories. The wisdom of Dickens and all Christmas storytellers." She seemed to pause for emphasis. "I love the sounds of this season. Even the sounds of this old house take on a different character at Christmas. These Victorian ladies seem to have a spirit all their own."

I heartily agreed but said nothing.

She reflected on the old home. "They don't build homes like this anymore. You've noticed the double set of doors in the front entryway?"

We both nodded in confirmation.

"In the old days—before the advent of the telephone . . ." She winked. "I'm an old lady," she confided, "I remember those days."

We smiled.

". . . Back in those days when people were receiving callers they would open the outer set of doors as a signal. And if the doors were closed it meant that they were not receiving callers. It seemed those doors were always open, all holiday long." She smiled longingly. "It seems silly now. You can imagine that the foyer was absolutely chilly." She glanced over to me. "Now I'm digressing. Tell us, Richard, which of the senses do you think are most affected by Christmas?"

I looked over at Keri. "The taste buds," I said flippantly. Keri rolled her eyes.

"No. I take it back. I would say the sense of smell. The smells of Christmas. Not just the food, but everything. I remember once, in grade school, we made Christmas ornaments by poking whole cloves into an orange. I remember how wonderful it smelled for the entire season. I can still smell it. And then there's the smell of perfumed candles, and hot wassail or creamy cocoa on a cold day. And the pungent smell of wet leather boots after my brothers and I had gone sledding. The smells of Christmas are the smells of childhood." My words trailed off into silence as we all seemed to be caught in the sweet glaze of Christmastime memories, and Mary nodded slowly as if I had said something wise.

◆

It was the sixth day of December. Christmas was only two and a half weeks away. I had already left for work and Keri had set about the rituals of the day. She stacked the breakfast dishes in the sink to soak, then descended the stairs to share in some conservation and tea with Mary. She entered the den where Mary read each morning. Mary was gone. In her chair lay the third Bible. Mary's Bible. Though we were aware of its existence, neither Keri nor I had actually ever seen it. It lay on the cushion spread open to the Gospel of John. Keri gently slipped her hand under the book's spine and lifted the text carefully. It was older than the other two Bibles, its script more Gothic and graceful. She examined it closely. The ink appeared marred, smeared by moisture. She ran a finger across the page. It was wet, moistened by numerous round drops. Tear drops. She delicately turned through the gold-edged pages. Many of the leaves were spoiled and stained from tears. Tears from years past, pages long dried and wrinkled. But the open pages were still moist. Keri laid the book back down on the chair and walked out into the hall. Mary's thick wool coat was missing from the lobby's crested hall tree. The inner foyer doors were ajar and at the base of the outer set of doors snow had melted and puddled on the cold marble floor, revealing Mary's departure. Mary's absence left Keri feeling uneasy. Mary rarely left the home before noon and, when she did, typically went to great lengths to inform Keri of the planned excursion days in advance. Keri went back upstairs until forty-five minutes later, when she heard the front door open. She ran down to meet Mary, who stood in the doorway, wet and shivering from the cold.

"Mary! Where have you been?" Keri exclaimed. "You look frozen!" Mary looked up sadly. Her eyes were swollen and red.

"I'll be all right," she said, then without an explanation disappeared down the hall to her room.

After brunch she again pulled on her coat to leave. Keri caught her in the hall on the way out. "I'll be going out again," she said simply. "I may return late."

"What time shall I prepare supper?" Keri asked.

Mary didn't answer. She looked directly at her, then walked out into the sharp winter air.

It was nearly half past eight when Mary returned that evening. Keri had grown increasingly concerned over her strange behavior and had begun looking out the balcony window every few minutes for Mary's return. I had already arrived home from work, been thoroughly briefed on the entire episode, and, like Keri, anxiously anticipated her return. If Mary had looked preoccupied before, she was now positively engrossed. She uncharacteristically asked to take supper alone, but then invited us to join her for tea.

"I'm sure my actions must seem a little strange," she apologized. She set her cup down on the table. "I've been to the doctor today, on account of these headaches and vertigo I've been experiencing."

She paused for an uncomfortably long period. I sensed she was going to say something terrible.

"He says that I have a tumor growing in my brain. It is already quite large and, because of its location, they cannot operate." Mary looked straight ahead now, almost through us. Yet her words were strangely calm.

"There is nothing that they can do. I have wired my brother in London. I thought you should know."

Keri was the first to throw her arms around Mary. I put my arms around the two of them and we held each other in silence. No one knew what to say.

◆

Denial, perhaps, is a necessary human mechanisim to cope with the heartaches of life. The following weeks proceeded largely without incident and it became increasingly tempting to delude ourselves into complacency, imagining that all was well and that Mary would soon recover. As quickly as we did, however, her headaches would return and reality would slap our faces as brightly as the frigid December winds. There was one other curious change in Mary's behavior. Mary seemed to be growing remarkably disturbed by my obsession with work and now took it upon herself to interrupt my endeavors at increasingly frequent intervals. Such was the occasion the evening that she asked the question.

"Richard. Have you ever wondered what the first Christmas gift was?"

Her question broke my engrossment in matters of business and weekly returns. I looked up.

"No, I can't say that I've given it much thought. Probably gold, frankincense, or myrrh. If in that order, it was gold." I sensed that she was unsatisfied with my answer.

"If an appeal to King James will answer your question, I'll do so on

Sunday," I said, hoping to put the question to rest. She remained unmoved.

"This is not a trivial question," she said firmly. "Understanding the first gift of Christmas is important."

"I'm sure it is, Mary, but this is important right now."

"No," she snapped, "you don't know what is important right now." She turned abruptly and walked from the room.

I sat quietly alone, stunned from the exchange. I put away the ledger and climbed the stairs to our room. As I readied for bed, I posed to Keri the question Mary had asked.

"The first gift of Christmas?" she asked sleepily. "Is this a trick question?"

"No, I don't think so. Mary just asked me and was quite upset that I didn't know the answer."

"I hope she doesn't ask me, then," Keri said, rolling over to sleep.

I continued to ponder the question of the first gift of Christmas until I gradually fell off in slumber. That night the angel haunted my dreams.

◆

The following morning at the breakfast table, Keri and I discussed the previous evening's confrontation.

"I think that the cancer is finally affecting her," I said.

"How is that?" Keri asked.

"Her mind. She's starting to lose her mind."

"She's not losing her mind," she said firmly. "She's as sharp as you or me."

"Such a strong 'no'," I said defensively.

"I'm with her all day. I ought to know."

"Then why is she acting this way? Asking weird questions?"

"I think she's trying to share something with you, Rick. I don't know what it is, but there is something." Keri walked over to the counter and brought a jar of honey to the table. "Mary is the warmest, most open individual I've ever met, except . . ." She paused. "Do you ever get the feeling that she is hiding something?"

"Something?"

"Something tragic. Terribly tragic. Something that shapes you and changes your perspective forever."

"I don't know what you're talking about," I said.

Suddenly Keri's eyes moistened. "I'm not so sure that I do either. But there is something. Have you ever seen the Bible that she keeps in the den?" I shook my head. "The pages are stained with tears." She turned away to gather her thoughts. "I just think that there is a reason that we're here. There is something she is trying to tell you, Rick. You're just not listening."

Chapter V

•

THE
STONE ANGEL

*M*y conversation with Keri had left me curious and bewildered. As I gazed outside at the snow-covered streets I saw Steve in his driveway brushing snow off his car. It occurred to me that he might have some answers. I ran upstairs to the Christmas Box, removed the first letter from it, and scrolled it carefully. Then stowing it in the inside pocket of my overcoat, I quietly slipped out of the house and crossed the street. Steve greeted me warmly.

"Steve, you've known Mary a long time."

"Pretty much all my life."

"There's something I want to ask you about."

He sensed the serious tone of my voice and set the brush down.

"It's about Mary. You know she's like family to us." He nodded in agreement. "There seems to be something troubling her, and we want to help her, but we don't know how. Keri thinks that she might be hiding something. If that's the case I think that I might have found a clue." I looked down, embarrassed by the letter I was holding. "Anyway, I found some letters in a box in the attic. I think they're love letters. I was hoping that you could shed some light on this."

"Let me see it," he said.

I handed the letter over. He read it, then handed it back to me.

"They are love letters, but not to a lover."

I must have looked perplexed.

"I think you should see something. I'll be over at Mary's Christmas Eve to visit. I'll take you then. It'll be around three o'clock. It will explain everything."

I nodded my approval. "That will be fine," I said. I shoved the letter back into my coat, then paused. "Steve, have you ever wondered what the first gift of Christmas was?"

"No. Why do you ask?"

"Just curious, I guess." I walked back to my car and drove off to work.

As had become the norm, it was a busy day spent helping brides-to-be match colorful taffeta swatches to formal-wear accessories; choose between ascot or band ties; pleated, French-cuffed shirts with wingtip collars or plain shirts with colorful ruffled dickies. I had just finished measuring and reserving outfits for a large wedding party. Upon receiving the required cash deposit from the groom,

I thanked them for their business, waved goodbye, and turned to help a young man who had stood quietly at the counter awaiting my attention.

"May I help you?" I asked.

He looked down at the counter, swaying uneasily. "I need a suit for a small boy," he said softly. "He's five years old."

"Very good," I said. I pulled out a rental form and began to write. "Is there anyone else in the party that will need a suit?"

He shook his head no.

"Is he to be a ring bearer?" I asked. "We'd want to try to match his suit to the groom's."

"No. He won't be."

I made a note on the form.

"All right. What day would you like to reserve the suit for?"

"We'd like to purchase the suit," he said solemnly.

I set the form aside. "That may not be in your best interest," I explained. "These young boys grow so fast. I'd strongly suggest that you rent."

He just nodded.

"I just don't want you to be disappointed. The length of the coat cannot be extended, only the sleeves and pant length. He may grow out of it in less than a year."

The man looked up at me, initiating eye contact for the first time. "We'll be burying him in it," he said softly.

The words fell like hammers. I looked down, avoiding the lifeless gaze of his eyes.

"I'm sorry," I said demurely. "I'll help you find something appropriate."

I searched through a rack of boys suits and extracted a beautiful blue jacket with satin lapels.

"This is one of my favorites," I said solemnly.

"It's a handsome coat," he said. "It will be fine." He handed me a paper with the boy's measurements.

"I'll have the alterations made immediately. It will be ready to be picked up tomorrow afternoon."

He nodded his head in approval.

"Sir, I'll see that the jacket is discounted."

"I'm very grateful," he said. He opened the door and walked out, blending in with the coursing river of humanity that filled the sidewalks at Christmas time.

◆

As I had spent the morning measuring out seams and checking the availabilities of jackets, Keri was busy at her own routine. She had fed, bathed, and dressed Jenna, then set to work preparing Mary's brunch. She poached an egg, then topped a biscuit with it, dressing it with a tablespoon of Hollandaise sauce. She took the shrieking teapot from the stove and poured a cup of peppermint tea, set it all on a tray, and carried it out to the dining room.

She called down the hall, "Mary, your brunch is ready."

She went back to the kitchen and filled the sink with hot, soapy water and began to wash the dishes. After a few minutes she toweled off her hands and walked back to the dining room to see if Mary needed anything. The food was untouched. Keri explored the den but the Bible lay untouched on its shelf. She checked the hall tree and found Mary's coat hanging in its usual place. She walked down to the bedroom and rapped lightly on the door.

"Mary, your brunch is ready."

There came no reply.

Keri slowly turned the handle and opened the door. The drapes were still drawn closed and the room lay still and dark. In the bed she could see the form lying motionless beneath the covers. Fear seized her. "Mary! Mary!" She ran to her side. "Mary!" She put her hand against the woman's cheek. Mary was warm and damp and breathing shallowly. Keri grabbed the telephone and called the hospital for an ambulance. She looked out the window. Steve's car was still in the driveway. She ran across the street and pounded on the door. Steve opened it, instantly seeing the urgency on Keri's face.

"Keri, what's wrong?"

"Steve! Come quick. Something is terribly wrong with Mary!"

Steve followed Keri back to the house and into the room where Mary lay delirious on the bed. Steve took her hand. "Mary, can you hear me?"

Mary raised a tired eyelid, but said nothing. Keri breathed a slight sigh of relief.

Outside, an ambulance siren wound down. Keri ran out to meet it and led the attendants down the dark hall to Mary's room. They lifted Mary into a gurney and carried her to the back of the vehicle. Keri grabbed Jenna and followed the ambulance to the hospital in Mary's car.

I met Keri and the doctor outside of Mary's hospital room. Keri had called me at work and I had rushed down as soon as I could.

"This is to be expected," the doctor said clinically. "She has been pretty fortunate up until today, but now the tumor has started to put pressure on vital parts of the brain. All we can do is try to keep her as comfortable as possible. I know that's not very reassuring, but it's reality."

I put my arm around Keri.

"Is she in much pain?" Keri asked.

"Surprisingly not. I would have expected more severe headaches. She has headaches, but not as acute as most. The headaches will continue to come and go, gradually becoming more constant. Coherency is about the same. She was talking this afternoon but there's no way of telling how long she'll remain coherent."

"How is she right now?" I asked.

"She's asleep. I gave her a sedative. The rush to the hospital was quite a strain on her."

"May I see her?" I asked.

"No, it's best that she sleep."

◆

That night the mansion seemed a vacuum without Mary's presence and, for the first time, we felt like strangers in somebody else's home. We ate a simple dinner, with little conversation, and then retired early, hoping to escape the strange atmosphere that had surrounded us. But even my strange dreams, to which I had grown accustomed, seemed to be affected. The music played for me again, but its tone had changed to a poignant new strain. Whether it had actually changed, or I, affected by the day's events, just perceived the alteration, I don't know, but like the siren's song, again it drew me to the Christmas Box and the next letter.

December 6, 1916

My Beloved One,

Another Christmas season has come. The time of joy and peace. Yet how great a void still remains in my heart. They say that time heals all wounds. But even as wounds heal they leave scars, token reminders of the pain. Remember me, my love. Remember my love.

◆

Sunday morning, Christmas Eve, the snow fell wet and heavy and had already piled up nearly four inches by afternoon when Steve met me near the mansion's front porch.

"How's Mary today?" he asked.

"About the same. She had a bad bout of nausea this morning but otherwise was in pretty good spirits. Keri and Jenna are still at the hospital with her now."

He nodded in genuine concern. "Well, let's go," he said sadly. "It will be good for you to see this."

We crossed the street and together climbed the steep drive to his home. Still unaware of our destination, I followed him around to his backyard. The yard was filled with large cottonwood trees and overgrown eucalyptus shrubs. It was well secluded by a high stone wall that concealed the cemetery I knew to be behind it.

"There's a wrought-iron gate behind those bushes over there," Steve said, motioning to a hedge near the wall. "About forty years ago the owner here planted that hedge to conceal the access to the cemetery. He was an older man and didn't like the idea of looking out into it each day. My family moved here when I was twelve years old. It didn't take us boys long to discover the secret gate. We hollowed out the hedge so that we could easily slip into the cemetery from it. We were frequently warned by the sexton never to play in the cemetery, but we did, every chance we got. We'd spend hours there," Steve confided. "It was the ideal place for hide-and-seek."

We reached the gate. The paint had chipped and cracked from the cold, rusted steel, but the gate remained strong and well secured. A padlock held it shut. Steve produced a key and unlocked the gate. It screeched as it swung open. We entered the cemetery.

"One winter day we were playing hide-and-seek about here. I was hiding from my friend when he saw me and started to chase. I ran though the snow up to the east end of the cemetery; it was an area where we never played. One of our friends swore he had heard the wailing of a ghost up there and we decided the place was haunted. You know how kids are."

I nodded knowingly as we trudged on through the deepening snow.

"I ran up through there," he said pointing to a clump of thick-stumped evergreens, "then up behind the mausoleum. There, as I crouched behind a tombstone, I heard the wailing. Even muffled in the snow it was heart-wrenching. I looked up over the stone. There was a statue of an angel about three feet high with outstretched wings. It was new at the time and freshly whitewashed. On the ground before it knelt a woman, her face buried in the snow. She was sobbing as if her heart were breaking. She clawed at the frozen ground as if it held her from something she wanted desperately—more than anything. It was snowing that day and my friend, following my tracks, soon caught up to me. I motioned to him to be quiet. For more than a half hour we sat there shivering and watching in silence as the snow completely enveloped her. Finally she was silent, stood up, and walked away. I'll never forget the pain in her face."

Just then I stopped abruptly. From a distance I could see the outspread wings of the weather-worn statue of an angel. "My angel," I muttered audibly. "My stone angel."

Steve glanced at me.

"Who was buried there?" I asked.

"Come see," he said, motioning me over.

I followed him over to the statue. We squatted down and I brushed the snow away from the base of the monument. Etched in the marble pedestal, above the birth and death dates, were just three words:

OUR LITTLE ANGEL

I studied the dates. "The child was only three years old," I said sadly. I closed my eyes and imagined the scene. I could see the woman, wet and cold, her hands red and snow bitten. And then I understood. "It was Mary, wasn't it?"

His response was slow and melancholy. "Yes. It was Mary."

The falling snow painted a dreamlike backdrop of solitude around us.

It seemed a long while before Steve broke the silence. "That night I told my mother what I had seen. I thought that I would probably get in trouble. Instead she pulled me close and kissed me. She said that I should never go back, that we should leave the woman alone. Until now, I never did go back. At least not to the grave. I did come close enough to hear her crying, though. It would tear me up inside. For over two years she came here every day, even in spring when the pouring rain turned the ground to mud."

I turned away from the angel, thrust my hands in my coat pockets, and started back in silence. We walked the entire distance to the house before either one of us spoke. Steve stopped at his back porch.

"The child was a little girl. Her name was Andrea. For many years Mary placed a wooden box on the grave. It resembles the boxes the wise men carry in Nativity scenes. My guess is it's the box you found with the letters."

I mumbled a thank you and headed for home alone. I unlocked the heavy front door and pushed it open. A dark silence permeated the mansion. I climbed the stairs to our quarters and then the attic, and for the first time I brought the Christmas Box out into the light. I set it on the hall floor and sat down beside it. In the light, I could see the truly exquisite craftsmanship of the box. The high polish reflected our surroundings and distorted the images, giving a graceful halo to the reflected objects. I removed the last letter.

December 6, 1920

My Beloved One,

How I wish that I might say these things to your gentle face and that this box might be found empty. Even as the mother of our Lord found the tomb they placed Him in empty. And in this there is hope, my love. Hope of embracing you again and holding you to my breast. And this because of the great gift of Christmas. Because He came. The first Christmas offering from a parent to His children, because He loved them and wanted them back. I understand that in ways I never understood before, as my love for you has not waned with time, but has grown brighter with each Christmas season. How I look forward to that glorious day that I hold you again. I love you, my little angel.

Mother

Chapter VI

◆

THE ANGEL

I set the letter back in the box and pulled my knees into my chest, burying my head into my thighs. My mind reeled as if in a dream, where pieces of the day's puzzle are unraveled and rewoven into a new mosaic, defying the improbability of the cut edges fitting. Yet they did fit. The meaning of Mary's question was now clear to me. The first gift of Christmas. The true meaning of Christmas. My body and mind tingled with the revelations of the day. Downstairs I heard the rustling of Keri's return. I walked down and helped her in.

"I came back to get Jenna some dinner," she said, falling into my arms.

"I am so exhausted," she cried. "And so sad."

I held her tightly. "How is she?"

"Not very good."

"Why don't you lie down, I'll put on some soup and get Jenna ready for bed."

Keri stretched out on the sofa while I dressed Jenna, fed her, then carried her downstairs to the den.

It was dark outside, and in absence of a fire, the room was bathed by the peaceful illumination of the Christmas tree lights. Strands flashed on and off in syncopation, casting shadows of different shapes and hues. I held Jenna in silence.

"Dad, is Mary coming home for Christmas?" she asked.

I ran a hand through my hair. "No, I don't think so. Mary is very sick."

"Is she going to die?"

I wondered what that meant to my little girl.

"Yes, honey. I think she will die."

"If she is going to die, I want to give her my present first."

She ran over to the tree and lifted a small, inexpertly wrapped package. "I made her an angel." With excitement she unveiled a petite cardboard angel constructed with tape, glue, and paper clips.

"Dad, I think Mary likes angels."

I started to sob quietly. "Yeah, I think she likes angels, too."

In the silence of the lights we faced the death of a friend.

In the outer hall I could hear the ringing of the telephone. Keri answered it, then found us downstairs.

"Rick, that was the hospital. Mary is dying."

I wrapped Jenna up warmly and set her in the car with Keri. We drove separately, so that one of us could bring Jenna home when the time came. We arrived at the hospital and together opened the door to Mary's room. The room was dimly illuminated by a single lamp. We could hear Mary's shallow breathing. Mary was awake and looked toward us.

Jenna rushed to the side of the reclining bed and, inserting her tiny hand through the side rails, pressed the little angel into Mary's hand.

"I brought you something, Mary. It's your Christmas present."

Mary slowly raised the ornament to her view, smiled, then squeezed the little hand tightly.

"Thank you, darling." She coughed heavily. "It's beautiful." Then she smiled into the little face. "You're so beautiful." She rubbed her hand across Jenna's cheek.

Painfully, she turned to her side and extended her hand to me.

I walked to her side and took it gently in mine.

"How do you feel, Mary?"

She forced a smile through the pain. "Do you know yet, Rick? Do you know what the first Christmas gift was?"

I squeezed her hand tightly.

"You do understand, don't you?"

"Yes. I understand now. I know what you were trying to tell me."

Tears started to fall down my cheeks. I took a deep breath to clear my throat.

"Thank you, Mary. Thank you for what you've given me."

"You found the letters in the Christmas Box?"

"Yes. I'm sorry that I read them."

"No, it's all right. I'm glad the letters were read. They were meant to be read." She fell silent for a moment.

"I'd like you to have the Christmas Box. It's my Christmas gift to you."

"Thank you. I will always treasure it." The room was quiet.

"Andrea waits," she said suddenly.

I smiled. "She has been very close," I said.

She smiled at me again, then lifted her eyes to Keri.

"Thank you for your friendship, dear. It has meant a lot to me."

"Merry Christmas, Mary," Keri said.

"God bless you, child," she said back lovingly. "Take good care of your little family." She looked at Keri thoughtfully. "You'll do fine."

Mary closed her eyes and lay back into her pillow. Keri's eyes watered as she lifted Jenna and carried her out of the room. I stayed behind, caressing the smooth, warm hands for the last time.

"Merry Christmas, Mary," I whispered. "We'll miss you."

Mary's eyes opened again. She leaned forward toward the foot of the bed. A smile spread across her face as a single tear rolled down her cheek. She said something too soft to hear. I leaned my ear near to her mouth. "My angel," she repeated. I followed her gaze to the foot of the bed but saw only the green cotton hospital gown draped over the end rail. I looked back at her in sadness. She was leaving us, I thought. It was then that I heard the music. The gentle, sweet tines of the Christmas Box. Softly at first, then as if to fill the entire room, strong and bright and joyful. I looked again at the weary face. It was filled with peace. Her deep eyes sparkled and the smile grew. Then I understood and I too smiled. Andrea had come.

◆

By the time I reached home it was well past midnight. Mary's brother had arrived from London and in deference I had left them alone to share the last few minutes together. Jenna had been put to bed and Keri, not knowing when I would return, had sadly laid the Christmas packages under the tree. I sat down in the rocker in front of the illuminated Christmas tree and lay my head in my hands. Somewhere between the angel and Mary's house I had figured it out. The first gift of Christmas. It just came. It came to my heart. The first gift of Christmas was love. A parent's love. Pure as the first snows of Christmas. For God so loved His children that He sent His son, that we might someday return to Him. I understood what Mary had been trying to teach me. I stood up and walked up the stairs where my little girl lay sleeping. I picked up her warm little body and, cradling her tightly in my arms, brought her back down to the den. My tears fell on her hair. My little girl. My precious little girl. How foolish I'd been to let her childhood, her fleeting, precious childhood slip away. Forever. In my young mind everything was so permanent and lasting. My little girl would be my little girl forever. But time would prove me wrong. Someday she'd grow up. Someday she'd be gone and I would be left with the memory of giggles and secrets I might have known.

Jenna took a deep breath and snuggled close for warmth. I held her little body tightly against mine. This was what it meant to be a father, to know that one day I would turn around and my little girl would be gone. To look upon the sleeping little girl and to die a little inside. For one precious, fleeting moment, to hold the child in my arms, and would that time stood still.

But none of that mattered now. Not now. Not tonight. Tonight Jenna was mine and no one could take this Christmas Eve away from me but me. How wise Mary had been. Mary, who knew the pain of a father sending his son away on that first Christmas morn, knowing full well the path that lay ahead. Mary understood Christmas. The tears in the Bible showed that. Mary loved with the pure, sweet love of a mother, a love so deep that it becomes the allegory for all other love. She knew that in my quest for success in this world I had been trading diamonds for stones. She knew, and she loved me enough to help me see. Mary had given me the greatest gift of Christmas. My daughter's childhood.

EPILOGUE

*I*t was around nine o'clock Christmas morning that Mary's brother called to tell us Mary was gone. The call found Keri and me holding each other on the couch in Mary's den, surrounded by the aftermath of Christmas giving. I lifted the Christmas Box down from the fireplace mantel where we had placed it in memory of Mary. I set the box near the hearth, then one by one, let the flames devour the letters as Keri watched in silent understanding. The Christmas Box was at last empty.

Mary was buried next to the small angel statue that she had so faithfully visited. In the course of our assisting in the burial arrangements, the funeral home had asked Keri what they should engrave on the headstone. "A loving mother," she said simply.

Every Christmas Eve, for as long as we lived in the valley, we returned to the grave and laid a white lily beneath the feet of the angel with outspread wings. Keri and I lived in the mansion for the space of several more Christmas seasons until the family decided to sell the estate, and we purchased a home in the southern end of the valley. In the years since, our family grew from three to six, and though the demands of providing for such a family oftentimes seemed endless, I never forgot the lessons I learned that Christmas with Mary.

And to this day, the Christmas Box remains a source of great joy to me. For though it appears empty, to me it contains all that Christmas is made of, the root of all wonder in a child's eyes, and the source of the magic of Christmases for centuries to come. More than giving, more than believing, for these are mere manifestations of the contents of that box. The sacred contents of that box are a parent's pure love for a child, manifested first by a Father's love for all His children, as He sacrificed that which He loved most and sent His son to earth on that Christmas day so long ago. And as long as the earth lives, and longer, that message will never die. Though the cold winds of life may put a frost on the heart of many, that message alone will shelter the heart from life's storms. And for me, as long as I live, the magic inside the Christmas Box will never die.

It never will.

In Memoriam

◆

The Angel statue, of which the author makes mention, was destroyed in 1984 by the great floods that came through the Salt Lake Valley.

A new Angel monument, in remembrance of all those who have lost children, was erected in the same Salt Lake City cemetery and dedicated December 6, 1994.

The author wishes to invite all those who find themselves in Salt Lake City to lay a white flower at the statue's base.

The address of the City Cemetery is:

City Cemetery
200 "N" Street
Salt Lake City, Utah 84103

Please send flowers to the attention of the City Sexton.

About the Author

◆

RICHARD PAUL EVANS, a former advertising executive, wrote *The Christmas Box* for his daughters. Encouraged by those who read the story, Evans went on to publish the tale on his own. Evans lives in Salt Lake City, Utah, with his wife, Keri, and their three daughters, Jenna, Allyson, and Abigail. He is currently working on his next novel.

If you would like to be informed of Richard Paul Evans' upcoming books and events in your area, please send your name and address to:

Richard Paul Evans
576 E. South Temple
Salt Lake City, Utah 84102